WIN◌   ◌GHT

Sandra Whiting

abuddhapress@yahoo.com

ISBN: 9798393477714

Alien Buddha Press 2023

The following is a poetic work of fiction. Any similarities to actual people, places, or events, unless deliberately expressed otherwise by the author are purely coincidental.

PROLOGUE

Cassie's eyes began to flutter, awakened by the bird outside her window.

It was Saturday. The best day of the week.

A smile spread across her face, while the familiar scent of fresh-off-the-griddle pancakes wafted across the room.

Pancakes, her favorite.

She was happy but not surprised. After all, it was her 13th birthday.

Cassie skipped down the stairs, eager to see what her family had planned. Birthdays were always treasured days in the Fowler home.

Weekends, nuggets of time carved away, just for them.

"Happy birthday to my now teenager!" shrieked Cassie's mom with excitement. She danced over, apron on and spatula in hand, to give Cassie a kiss on the cheek.

"I love you, baby girl. Even if you *are* a teenager, you're still my baby girl."

"Hey, there she is!"

Dad barreled into the room with his larger-than-life personality.

"Happy birthday, kiddo."

"Thanks, guys."

Cassie quickly tore off the corner of a pancake and snuck it into her mouth. Courtney and Jeremy, Cassie's younger brother and sister, came bounding into the room.

"We saw that!"

"Saw what?" asked Cassie innocently, winking at her brother and sister as she quietly stole bits for them, too.

"We *all* saw that," said Dad, though not in a disapproving tone.

Everyone sat down at the table.

"So, what does the birthday girl want to do on her special day?"

All eyes on Cassie. Jeremy and Courtney, just as excited for the day ahead as her.

Cassie looked around the table. She really didn't care. So much love stared back at her. She was just happy to celebrate another birthday with her beloved family.

1.

Beep, beep, beep

The alarm
cut through
the room
like a sharp knife
slashing
through dense air.

I look
out my window
and up
towards the sky.

Bleak and gloomy,
a permanent gray.

A regular
occurrence
over
the past year.

I inhale my surroundings,
then exhale a sigh
so heavy
it sounds as if
the weight of the World
were just expelled
all at once,
wondering why
I should expect anything else.

It was better to accept reality for what it was.

Better to not think of some
fairy tale
of blue skies,
bluebirds,

happy holidays and
home-cooked meals.

2.

I put on
my favorite pair
of
ripped jeans,
a steal
from the local
Goodwill,
and one of
my younger sister
Courtney's
too-tight shirts -
even for her.

Thankfully,
due to the current fashion trend
I can pretend
as if
it's a crop top.
Next,
I reach
for my favorite cover -

Dad's plaid shirt,
of course.

That shirt -

Warm

Comforting

It reminds me of a sweeter time.

A time
when people
spoke
the name "Cassie"
and actually cared

what I had to say.

A time
when
I
actually cared
what they
had to say
in return.

A time
where there was
enjoyment and wonder.

A time not like now.

3.

Down the hall I go,
past my
brother
who has his
headset on again.

I'm just a shadow.

A nothing.

Unless part of his
imaginary,
limitless,
gaming World.

But why shouldn't I be?

Wasn't he invisible, too?

4.

I walk downstairs,
slowly,
as if I'm walking
to my demise.

Once excited for what stood at the bottom.

Now,
dreading what I might find.
The dishes are stacked
like a mountain
in the sink.
Bread crumbs
form a trail from
the overflowing garbage can,
and the only sounds
I can hear
are the thoughts
swirling in my head.

No breakfast.

Someone has to take out the trash.
Guess it's going to be me.

When does the bus come, again?

Cuz' it
looks like
I won't be getting
a ride
from Mom.

Speaking of Mom,
where is she?

Now I stop my thoughts.

I already know the answer.

5.

School is OK.

I'm definitely
not part of
the
"in" crowd,
but that doesn't matter to me.

Or does it?

I sit with the thought
for a moment
and decide
I have bigger things to worry about,
like if Mrs. Smith
will notice
I didn't do the readings
or even worse,
that I'm wearing the same outfit
from two days ago.

Later that day,
I meet up
with Maddie and Rachel
at lunch.

We laugh
and talk about things
kids our age
should -

Boys

The homecoming dance

School football team

For a second,

it almost feels like
the time known as
"before."

Then the bell rings,
and it reminds me
I'm one period closer
to returning to
that hellhole
others act
like
I'm supposed to love.

6.

Science is next.
I usually zone out.

Why should I care
about rock formations
or the life cycle
of some insect
that's just a
smaller version
of me?

I can tell
you
about the
"life cycle"
in the real World.

You're born

You hunt for food

You eat

You try to survive the best you can

You die

Whoop-de-doo.

Tell me something new,
and maybe
I'll look up
from my doodles
long enough
to
feign interest.

7.

I'm back at
"Home, Sweet Home"
but there's
nothing
sweet
about it.

Not anymore.

Mom's still not here.
Jeremy's gaming again.
Did he even go to school?

Mom doesn't care,
so why should I?

Courtney's putting on
red lipstick
and prancing around
in a shirt
even shorter
than my so-called
"crop top."

I wonder where she found the lipstick
or who she's putting it on for,
but not enough
to stop and ask.

I slam my
bedroom door shut
for privacy.
Not like anyone would come in,
anyways.

I look out the window.

It's starting to rain,

but the sky is still gray.

No rainbow today.

What's new....

Today
was a day
like
any other.

8.

The alarm sounds,
loud,
abruptly waking me
from the only place
I dare let myself dream -
my actual dreams.

Ironic, isn't it?

I look out the window,
a glutton for punishment.

Take a guess at the color.

There is one surprise.
Mom's car
is back
in the driveway.
I wander
down the stairs
after getting
myself dressed.

"Cassie, is that you?"

She's lying
on the couch,
and her voice sounds
as if
she just woke up.

"Hey, Mom. How are you feeling?"

"I'm here. I missed you, sweetie."

She says the right words,
but I don't think
she means them.

"I missed you, too."

I say the right words,
and I know
I don't mean them.

9.

I try
not to
blame her.

Dad was her rock.

At first the meds were just to cope.
After all,
she had three children to care for.

Childhood sweethearts,
retirement plans,
the small amount of savings
they had accumulated -
all ripped away by the "c" word.
The one that everyone knows
but dares not speak.

We never had much,
but we had love and each other.

That was enough for Mom.

It was enough for all of us.

10.

I know
she's hurting,
but I can't help
be mad.

Shouldn't I also be allowed to hurt?
Time to heal?
He was my dad.

Sometimes I wish the roles were reversed.

Here they are
again,
those thoughts,
cutting through the space
that creates
an ocean
between us.

I give her an aspirin
and a bottle of water.

She gives me a kiss.

Maybe someday the ocean will become a lake.

11.

Back in science,
Mr. Johnson has a
new topic
for today.

"Metamorphosis," he declares,
as if he's
going to give us
some
profound
life-changing
lesson.

I continue to doodle as usual.

"Does anyone know what this word means?"

I roll my eyes.
Of course Mary raises her hand.

"Metamorphosis is changing from one form or object into another."

"Very good," says Mr. Johnson.

She cocks her head sideways
and smiles.

I let out
a sarcastic groan.
What should she know about metamorphosis?
It's not like
she would want
things to change -
not when she's dating the captain of the football team,
is head cheerleader
and class valedictorian.

"Cassie, do you have something you'd like to add?"

Crap.

Did everyone hear that?

"Nope,"
I say shortly,
looking back down
at my paper.

My eyes fix on the page,
blocking out
anything
or anyone else
in my
line of vision.

My ears,
the only one of my senses engaged.

Transformation,
changing into something or somebody else.

Now that's something I could get on board with.

12.

Back in my room,
I decide
to look through
my bag
and attempt
some of my
class assignments.

Mr. Johnson
and his talk of metamorphosis
was somewhat intriguing.

More exciting than my actual life.

I just can't seem to escape that word

      - metamorphosis -

It seems to float
into thin air
and fly away,
almost as if
it has a life of its own.

Maybe someday I'll fly away, too.

13.

Metamorphosis
is an
interesting concept,
but a lesson
on
butterflies?

Sounds like a unit I should have completed in the second grade.

I flip the page
with a decided eye roll.
Seems kinder than the types of words
that are
rolling
off my tongue
these days.

Great - a project.

Good ol' dependable,
predictable
Mr. Johnson.

Metamorphosis, for him, a familiar word but foreign concept.

14.

For the next two months we will learn all about butterflies. The life cycle, different species, colors, locations around the World and more. For your final assignment, you will be required to write an essay about a butterfly of your choice. Further directions will be provided at a later date.

A key theme to coincide with this unit is that of metamorphosis - how it relates to the life of the butterfly and life, in general. I want you to start to think about the World around you. You are an integral part of society, a life-beating force. Over the coming weeks, we will merge nature with science and perhaps, butterflies won't be the only thing you learn along the way.

15.

Beep, beep, beep

Same
loud,
annoying
alarm.

Same
time.

Same
gray morning.

Days around here
are often gray,
but it is especially true
of March
in Western, NY.

I repeat the same process
as the previous two mornings.

Surprises
a thing of the past.

The only unknown,
whether or not Mom
will be there
when I go
downstairs.

Consistently inconsistent.

This time, she's up.
She puts a glass of milk on the table and cracks a half smile,
not sure where to begin
and full of disappointment.

She's trying.

I return the smile,
feeling the exact same way.

Only the disappointment is not mine to own.

16.

I step off the bus,
look at the school
and take a deep breath
of that
cool,
March air.

Maybe not everything about March is gloomy.
I do like the crisp cold,
that feeling of spring
just around the corner.

Maybe it's
my mood
that's making things
appear
grayer than they
really are.

Then again,
maybe not.

I've now reached the front steps.

Ready for the day to begin
and surprisingly,
ready to learn about butterflies.

17.

A packet
gets passed
down the row.
It finally reaches me.

An introduction to 5 common butterflies:

1. Cabbage White
2. Orange Sulfur
3. Painted Lady
4. Monarch
5. Viceroy

Mr. Johnson's lips begin to move.

I have every intention of listening,
though of course
I won't
show it.

A story begins
to take shape
in my mind.
The butterfly names
start to come alive
on the page,
painting the type of
un-fairy tale story
that has become
my new reality.

"The *cabbage, white* in color, reminds me of the *orange sulfur* smell
coming out of our broken-down faucet. Perhaps I can pretend I'm no
longer here. Just a figment of someone's imagination, like the *painted
lady* in a portrait that belongs to some rich *monarch*.

Maybe some *vices* are too big for one person to overcome alone."

RING!

Class is over.

With a sudden jolt
I'm thrust
back
into reality.

Did I ever really leave?

18.

Back home,
it's the usual scene.

Mom's asleep.
It's 3 o'clock in the afternoon.

I go upstairs
to look at
our first butterfly assignment.

I still can't seem to shake "metamorphosis."

Change

New beginnings

Hope

I haven't allowed myself to use that word since the "before" time.

Desire

Aspiration

Dream

...but never hope.

19.

Science homework.

I wonder if
home
is
work
for anyone else.

Population, location.

Blah, blah, blah

Appearance, feeding.

Blah, blah, blah

Thought question.

What's that?

Look,
I'm already thinking.

*Thought question: Take a closer look at the word "butterfly."
Examine the different meanings of the word. Which ones stand out?
Can you relate to the word "butterfly" in any way?*

Perhaps Mr. Johnson isn't as predictable as I thought.

20.

I type the words
"Butterfly Definition"
into
my phone.

What else do I have to do?

Try to wake Mom up?
Cook myself some dinner?
Attempt to pull Jeremy from VR?

No thank you -
there's always tomorrow for that.

21.

but·ter·fly
[ˈbədərˌflī]
NOUN
butterfly (noun) · *butterflies (plural noun)* · *butterfly stroke (noun)*
   1. a nectar-feeding insect with two pairs of large, typically
      brightly colored wings that are covered with microscopic
      scales. Butterflies are distinguished from moths by having
      clubbed or dilated antennae, holding their wings erect when
      at rest, and being active by day.
         o   having a two-lobed shape resembling the spread
             wings of a butterfly:
             "a butterfly clip"
   2. a showy or frivolous person:
      "a social butterfly"
   3. *informal*
      (butterflies)
      a fluttering and nauseous sensation felt in the stomach
      when one is nervous.
      synonyms:
      nervousness · nerves · fit of
      nerves · edginess · uneasiness · anxiety · anxiousness · tens
      ion · agitation · fretfulness · restlessness · fidgeting · tremb
      ling · shaking · jumpiness · stage fright · buck fever · Joe
      Blakes · worriment
      antonyms:
      calmness · serenity
   4. a stroke in swimming in which both arms are raised out of
      the water and lifted forwards together.
VERB
butterfly (verb) · *butterflies (third person present)* · *butterflied (past
tense)* · *butterflied (past participle)* · *butterflying (present participle)*
   1. split (a piece of meat or fish) almost in two and spread it
      out flat:
      "butterfly the shrimp using a small sharp knife"

37

22.

Well,
I can forget about Number 2.

I'm not a mute,
but I'm certainly
not a
"social butterfly."
I'll save that one for
know-it-all
Mary.

Number 3: "Butterflies in your stomach."

Nerves.

A sick feeling.

Number 3 I can relate to.

Number 3 reminds me of Dad's cancer diagnosis.

Maybe it's
more appropriate
for me to just say
Dad,
as a whole.

When I say
Dad,
it makes me feel
like the
whole thing
is tied up neatly with a bow
and tucked away
in some corner
of my room.

Not my reality,

which is more reminiscent of
scraps of paper
strewn about
in a
windstorm.

23.

Are nerves butterflies?

I forgot about the term
"butterflies in your stomach."
That's what happens
when you're
always on
autopilot.

You lose track of what's normal and what's not.

To tell you the truth,
I'm not even sure
what I'm
nervous about.

What's to come?
What won't?

That things can never go back to the way they were?

That *I*
can never go back
to the way
I was?

I decide on all of the above.

24.

To my surprise,
the sun is
slightly
shining,
       or at least it's not a slate gray.

Also to my surprise,
Jeremy is eating breakfast at the table.

Courtney's grabbing
some juice
and being, well,
all *Courtney.*

Mom is putting bread in the toaster.

Something's up.
Something's always up
when we're together like this.

"Oh, good, you're here. How'd you sleep?"

She doesn't wait
long enough
for me
to answer.

"Mommy has to go away for a while."

      Hasn't she been away this whole time?

"It won't be too long. Mommy will be back before you know it."

I wish
she would
stop
calling herself
 "Mommy."

"Mommy"
implies an innocence,
a warm figure
offering protection
and love.

I wish she wouldn't use that word.
It doesn't fit her anymore.

"Jeremy, I need you to do something for me."

Jeremy
seems to be
even less interested
in this conversation
than me.

"Jeremy, are you listening to me? Look at me."

He whips up his head,
eyes lashing out
in
anger.

Whoa.

Jeremy is listening.
He's mad.
Angry.

Those eyes,
as if they
could pierce
right
through her.

But more than that,
I see sadness.
The longing for what we once had,

what we all took for granted.

Our regrets replay
day in
       and
day out,
like a record player
that just won't stop.

For the first time in months, I feel sorry for him.

He claps back.
       "What do you have to tell me that I don't already know?"
Enough disdain
that even Courtney
looks up
from her phone.

"I know you're mad, and I'm sorry. I'm trying."

     Is she?

"Jeremy, while I'm gone, I need you to be the man of the house."

My stomach does somersaults.

The man of the house was Dad,
should still be Dad.

Number 3

Were these butterflies?

They are more than butterflies now.
I feel a fire
in my stomach
that could
rival
Hades.

"Are you kidding me!?"

I burst in,
unable to restrain myself.

"Man of the house!? For one thing, he's barely 11 and for another,
he can barely take care of himself, let alone us. The man of the house
was Dad. It should have always been Dad! And then when it was no
longer Dad, it should have been YOU!"

It's as if
a chest full of rage
buried deep
below the Earth
was coming to the surface.

"Cassie, I'm just saying that.."

"NO! Stop talking! You talk and talk and talk. The same words over
and over again. But you never DO! Don't tell me how sorry you are or
how much you'll miss us - I don't believe it."

"Cassie, please. I'm sorry. I just don't know what else to say."

Tears start to stream down her face.

Tears are rolling down mine.

"Good-bye, Mom. Have a great trip," I say, grabbing an untoasted slice
of bread off the counter.

And just like that
I walk away,
creating an
even bigger space
between us
than there
already
was.

Metamorphosis.

Damn Mr. Johnson and his stupid butterflies.

25.

I'm still bothered
by the events
of the morning
when I
get to
science class.

I take my seat
next to
Maddie and Rachel
and pick up my pen
to doodle.

Now it's not the words
but rather my pen that
seems to come alive.
I find myself
making
gentle strokes
on the page
that transform into
beautiful
dancing
butterflies,
and my mind
dances away
with them.

I used to
love the outdoors,
especially
during spring.
I'd play outside
for hours,
my cue to go in
when the sun
began
to fall.

46

I'd marvel at the
pops of green
sprouting from the dirt,
excited
for what
new
hidden treasures
would be unearthed
for our pleasure.

Spring in Western, NY can be gray
but also vibrant.

Meaningful.

I suppose,
like everything,
it depends
on your
outlook.

Mr. Johnson is right.
I've already
learned
something.

I miss spring and all that it entails.

26.

I step
off the bus
and drift
into the house.
Our neighbor,
Mrs. Lee,
grabbed the mail
and left a small dinner.
Nothing fancy
but enough
to get by
for the night.

Looks like Mom didn't
completely
forget about us.

I grab a Slim Jim from the pantry
and head upstairs
to pull out
my definition sheet.

Number 4

The butterfly stroke.

I don't know much about swimming.
Maddie,
Rachel
and I
used to go to the
community
swimming pool -
mainly just to flirt with boys.
I learned to swim
but not very well.
The only time
I'd ever heard of

the butterfly stroke
was during the Olympics.

I guess
Number 4
joins Number 2
on my
possible paths
to self-discovery.

Number 3 stands alone.

Maybe that's why I can relate.

27.

Days turn into weeks,
and I almost
don't even notice.

I wake
to the sound of
rain
hitting my window,
slapping me into reality.

Gray and rainy.
Welcome to
April
in Western, NY.

Mrs. Lee is now a house guest,
though a quiet one at that.

Guess she figured someone needed to watch over us.
What a novel idea.

Mr. Johnson and his butterflies
have taken
a
back seat.

I pretend I don't care that Mom's gone,
but where is she?
I'm starting to wonder
if she's
ever
coming back.

Do I miss her?

Loaded question.

Enough ammo to pack a gun,

with the same
kickback
after pulling
the trigger.

I decide I do. But why?

How can I
hate someone
and miss them
all
at the
same time?

Butterflies

Verb

Split in two

I leap up the stairs,
two at a time,
and fumble through
the stack of papers
just sitting
on my
desk.

Unloved
and
unattended.

Funny.

Perhaps life
is a cycle,
and we do unto others
what's been done
unto us.

Maybe that cycle can be broken.

I mean,
who would have thought
I'd be
missing
Mom?

I pretend I don't care,
but the truth is
I do.

I care about Jeremy.
I care about Courtney and her lipstick.
I care about
Mom,
her whereabouts,
and if
we'll ever be
as close
as we once
were,
and
I care about Mr. Johnson
and those
damn
butterflies.

Metamorphosis.

Back with all
its mysterious
intrigue.

28.

Verb: To split in two and spread it out flat

I'm mad.

Mad at Mom.

Mad at Dad.

Mad at Me.

Mad at the World.

But I'm also
tired,
and
I miss
seeing
Mom's face,
as infrequent as it was.

Emotions bleed
one into the next,
and I like this feeling
even less
than when I had
no
feelings
at all.

29.

Maddie and Rachel are waiting for me at my locker.

"Hey, girl. We're going to the creek after school. Mitch, Benny and Michael are probably stopping by, too! You in?"

Normally,
I'd be giddy
with
excitement.

Boys

The creek

Normalcy

But today
I just want to go home
and see
if there is any word
from Mom.
Not that I would
tell Maddie and Rachel,
of course.

I decide
to
play it cool.

"Man! I would totally be there, but I have to watch Jeremy. This sucks!"

Blame it on
Jeremy,
that works.

"Seriously!? You can't find someone else?"

"Nah, I wish I could. Mom has to work late tonight, so I've got to get dinner ready. Sorry guys. Text me and let me know how it goes."

I still haven't told them Mom's gone.

Maybe I should say
"missing"
at this point.
Saying she's working late
is easier,
less heavy.
An unwanted burden
left solely
for me.

Definitely working late.

Not unknown fate.

30.

Mr. Johnson
stops me
after class.

"Cassie,
how is
your butterfly assignment
going?"

What.

Is.

Happening.

Mr. Johnson
has never
stopped me
before today.
Can he tell I'm faking my indifference?

"It's OK," I answer shortly, not sure how to respond.

"I've seen some of your drawings on the corner of your assignments.
You're a very talented artist."

I feel my cheeks flush.

"Thanks."

"How's your mother these days? I haven't seen her at church?"

It's like he knows.

"She's OK. Keeping busy."

Keeping busy
or busy keeping

away
from us?

Either will suffice.

Mr. Johnson
looks
at me.
The silence between us,
somehow filled with
unspoken words.

I move closer
to the door.

Uncomfortable
to my core.

"Have you taken a look at the thought questions yet? Some of your
classmates have started to take an interest in them."

Should I tell him the truth?
I actually
do find
the project
somewhat
intriguing.

This conversation? Not so much.

"I've looked at it a little."

He gives me
that look
again.

"OK. Well, let me know if you ever want to discuss the project any
further. You can always stop by."

Mr. Johnson appears

to have taken
an interest
in me.
I don't know
how I feel about it.
It's been a while
since
anyone cared
what I had
to think.

Split in two.

I say
thanks
as I awkwardly walk
to my
next class,
deciding to
add
the definition
to
Number 3.

31.

Mrs. Lee
is wiping down
the kitchen counters
when I
walk through
the door.

She's an old widow.
I wonder if
she's
now
one of the forgotten,
like me.

"Hey, Mrs. Lee."

More uncomfortableness.

Why was I
suddenly making
an attempt
to talk to
her?

Why did
Mr. Johnson
suddenly
make an attempt
to talk to
me?

Thoughts
swirl around my head
like a cyclone,
breaking down
every barrier
I once
built.

"Cassie, dear. How was school?"

Was Mrs. Lee
actually
asking me
about my
day?
Did she just
call me
dear?

"It was OK. How was yours?"

"Same as usual. When you're all by yourself, there's not much to do.
But that's not for you to worry about."

Little
did she
know.

Worry

Nerves

Number 3

I decide
to get her
a glass
of water.
Makes me feel
like
Mom's here,
though
I don't need
to grab
the pills.

"Mrs. Lee, - *no matter the circumstance, Mom and Dad always taught us to address people as "Mr." and "Mrs."* - don't you miss being at your house? Won't someone be wondering where you are?"

It sounds rude,
but I don't mean it to be.

"No one seems to worry much about an old widow like myself. No children to call on, and no man to come home to. But enough about me. What did you learn in school today?"

I surprise myself
by sitting down
beside her,
aware that
this is the first time
anyone's
asked me
what I learned
in school
since "before".

Courtney walks in.
She glances over,
enough interest
to take her away
from her phone
for 2 seconds
but not enough
to sit down.

"Just the usual," I say.

I haven't talked
to anyone
about
my butterfly assignment,
yet
for some reason
I feel safe

with Mrs. Lee.
It's an
old,
comfortable
feeling
I didn't
realize
how much
I missed
until
right this second.

"We do have kind of a cool assignment in science class. It's about butterflies. All the usual things you'd expect. Learning about the different types of butterflies, their life cycles...ya know, science stuff. What's kinda cool are the thought questions my teacher adds each day."

I don't tell her
I'm still on
Question 1.

"What sort of questions does he or she ask?"

"Well, our first one had to do with the different definitions of the word "butterfly" and seeing if any resonate with us."

"Hmm. Sounds interesting. Any strike a chord so far?"

Jeremy walks in
and looks at us
with a
peculiar face.
As much as I've
reluctantly
enjoyed
talking with
Mrs. Lee,
I'm relieved.

I'm not ready
to tell her about
Number 3,
though something inside
tells me
I will.

32.

I head upstairs
and take out
my homework.

I'm not sure
if it's
Mr. Johnson's surprise ambush
or
Mrs. Lee's inquisition,
but I have
a renewed desire
to work on
my
butterfly project.
I review
my answers
so far.
Not good enough
to warrant
A's
but likely C's
or even
a B.

Average.

Just like me.

I look at the first definition again:

>*A nectar-feeding insect with two pairs of large, typically brightly colored wings that are covered with microscopic scales. Butterflies are distinguished from moths by having clubbed or dilated antennae, holding their wings erect when at rest, and being active by day.*

Nectar feeding insect

Brightly colored wings

Microscopic scales

Distinguished from moths

Wings erect when at rest

Active by day

Ding.

It's Maddie.
Suddenly
the creek,
Benny
and an
afternoon of play
seem like nothing
compared to

Mrs. Lee's Lonely Life

My Missing Mom

My Dead Dad and

Cautiously Caring Cassie

Split in two.

33.

Beep, beep, beep

I flop over
and smack
the snooze button,
hoping
for
a few more minutes
of solitude
and peace.

That smell.

Pancakes?

Couldn't be.
That was only
during
the
"before."

I get up, my curiosity getting the better of me.

Wobbling down
the stairs,
still
in my favorite
faded t-shirt and boy shorts,
I see Jeremy
at the table
and Mrs. Lee
at the stove.

"Morning, Cas."

Cas?
No one's
ever

called me
Cas.
But I suppose
when
you've been alone
for as long
as Mrs. Lee,
no friends' names to shorten,
no family to wait on,
Cas means more
than just those
three
letters.

It means someone to care about,
someone who might care about you.

It has meaning.

I
gave
her meaning,
and
suddenly

Cas had meaning to me.

34.

"Morning, Mrs. Lee."

Jeremy
looks up at me
with a
smile.

"Hi, Cas."

He seems to like it, too.

"Hey, Jerm."

We both giggle.
A forgotten,
foreign
sound,
and in
this
moment -

The most beautiful sound I have ever heard.

35.

Jeremy and I
walk into
school together.

I can't help
but notice
the World seems
a little livelier.

The grass
has a greener hue,
flowers begin to emerge
and the sky
has a touch
of blue.

I think my theory may be right.

Outlook begets environment.

Or does environment beget one's outlook?

I suppose
both
are true,
but I'm beginning to realize
that
perhaps the World
isn't as gray
as it once
appeared.

36.

Today
Mr. Johnson is focusing
on the
viceroy butterfly,
which mimics
the monarch.

I had never
heard
of the viceroy butterfly,
let alone pronounce it,
until today.

Vice-roy

Vices come to mind.

Maybe
that's because
the concept
is
all
too
familiar.

Someone else
in a
less dysfunctional family
might think of
Vice President or Vice Principal,
but not me.

I like the viceroy.

I understand the viceroy.

The mimic

The impersonator

Sometimes
it's easier
to mimic others
than
really
get to know
yourself.

Is that what Mom is doing?

Dysfunctional -
yes.
But is it
easier
for her to be
someone else,
even if that
someone
is constantly disappointed
and disappointing
others?

Easier than to actually know herself?

To face
reality,
that she is
now a single mom
with three children
who are not only
angry at the World
but angry
at
her?

For the
first time
in what feels like

a
lifetime,
I feel sorry for her.

The bell rings again.
I leave class
and blend
into a sea of people
who have no idea
the depths
of my pain.
They see a
poor,
jaded
teenager
who seems
to hate
the World.

In reality,
she just feels like
she can barely
get her head
above water
and is screaming for
someone,
anyone,
to throw her a raft
bring her to shore
and breathe
some life
into her
again.

37.

Mrs. Lee
has her
feet up on the coffee table,
TV on
and remote in hand
when I walk
through
the door.

Making herself
at home
and
building
one
for us.

"Hi there, Miss Cas. How are you feeling today?"

"Hi, Mrs. Lee," I say with a smile. I'm actually happy to see her. "It was good. Hung out with the girls. The usual stuff."

"That's good. You should be hanging with the girls, talking about boys and other things girls your age do. Sit with me for a minute, will you?"

"Sure," I say, slowly lowering myself onto the couch.

"Tell me about your brother and sister."

What's there to tell?
Jeremy
escapes reality
because
he'd rather live
anywhere
than here
and Courtney,
well,
I don't know about her.

She doesn't seem
to care
to be
a part of
this family,
only cares
about her friends.
Who could blame her?

"Well, Jeremy has always been into gaming but that's all he does since
Dad passed, and Courtney is glued to her phone. I couldn't tell you any
more about her than what you already see."

"Hmmmm," said Mrs. Lee, shaking her head in that disapproving yet
pitying way people do when they are judging and feeling sorry for you,
all at the same time. "Cassie, dear. We need to talk. I got a letter from
your Mom today."

My eyes widen,
and butterflies
once again
do somersaults
in my stomach -
waiting
for the
impending doom
I'd started
to
forget.

38.

A lump forms in my throat.

My mouth,
so dry
I can't even speak
the words
at first.

Maybe it's because I'm afraid of the answer.

"What did she say? Is she coming back?"

It's only been
about a month
and a half.
Doesn't seem
that long
in the grand scheme of things,
but a month and a half
of not knowing
where your mom is -

If she abandoned you.
If she's even alive.

Seems like an eternity.

"She is," said Mrs. Lee. "She's getting the help she needs. Your mom
has been ill for a long time. Not in the way your dad was, but a sickness
just the same. She met up with an old friend who helped check her into
a really nice place. She misses you all so much, but she needs to get
herself better first. She's afraid if she comes back, she won't have the
strength to leave you again. That's why she hasn't returned. She's so
sorry and hopes you understand."

"Mmhmm."

I nod my head in agreement,

an instinctual defense
since
Dad died.

Who cares about my opinion, anyways?

I'm glad
she's getting help,
but how could she
do this
to us?

Not knowing
if we are
going to have
a parent anymore -
again.

She KNOWS what that did to us last time.

What it did to me.

Look what it did to her.

39.

A week more
has passed,
and I still haven't
fully processed
Mom's letter.

I'm glad
she's getting clean,
I hope,
and I really like
having
Mrs. Lee
here.

She's calming.

We are
all starting
to get into
a routine.

I think Mrs. Lee likes being here, too.

"Morning, lovelies!"

This is how she greets us.

We all take a seat
at the table.
Even Courtney.
Mrs. Lee
insists
we start the day
this way.
Breakfast all together as a family, and
always
with a glass
of orange juice.

"A day without orange juice is like a day without sunshine."

I like that saying
and think
perhaps she's right.
My days have
certainly
become sunnier.
I'm starting to awaken
along with
the Earth.

It feels good to no longer be in hibernation.

40.

One period rolls into the next.
Except this time,
I'm not dreading
what the final bell
signifies.

"Hi, Mr. Johnson," I say, heading into class.

"Cassie," he says approvingly.

I take
my usual seat
by Maddie and Rachel.
I open up my notebook.

Daydreams and doodles
replaced by
interest and intrigue.

We learn more about the viceroy.

Like that its flight,
unlike that
of the monarch butterfly,
is actually fast
and more
erratic.

Like holding on for dear life.

I think I
could have been
a viceroy
in a
past life.

Maybe that's why I'm so good at it now.

41.

This time,
I surprise Mr. Johnson
with the ambush
at the end
of class.

"Hey, Mr. Johnson."

"Hi, Cassie. Is there something I can help you with?"

Nervously I respond, "Um, yeah. I'm actually wondering if you know when we will start to see butterflies around here."

"Well, it depends which butterflies you are looking for."

"The viceroy."

I'm decisive in my response.
So decisive
it slightly surprises
Mr. Johnson.
He doesn't ask why,
and I'm grateful
for that.

"Around here, the viceroys usually come in late spring or early summer."

"Thanks, Mr. Johnson."

I'm already halfway to the door when he says, "Cassie, did you know they sell butterfly kits at the store? You can care for the butterflies yourself and set them free."

I did not.

Number 3 -
there they are again in all their glory.

"Oh really?" I ask nonchalantly. "I didn't know that. Thanks for letting me know. I'll see ya tomorrow."

We flash a half-smile at each other.
I walk
towards the door
and pause
at its edge,
as if stepping
over the threshold
and into the hall
will signify
a new World.

There's no going back.

Holding my breath,
I leave the room.

I can live with that.

42.

"Hi-yah, Mrs. Lee!"

I skip
through the door
with more
pep in my step
than I've had
in months.

"Hi-yah yourself, Miss Cas. How was your day?"

I've gotten used to hearing those
wonderful,
meaningful,
four little words.

In an upbeat tone I respond, "Good. Remember when I told you we've
been learning about butterflies?"

"Mmmmhmmm," she says while pulling out two glasses from the
cupboard.

"Well, I've become pretty interested in the project. Did you know that
the orange and black butterflies we see outside during the summer
might not be monarchs? There's one that looks just like the monarch
butterfly. It's called the viceroy. It mimics the monarch, but if you look
closely at it, there is a black stripe across the wing and its flight is more
erratic."

"Is that right?" asks Mrs. Lee, pouring two glasses of orange juice and
gesturing for me to sit.

"Yeah, and did you know that you can buy butterflies? Like me and
you can just go and buy them! I knew the science teachers got them
from somewhere and that they had museums for butterflies, but I never
knew someone like me or you could just go to the store and bring them
home."

"That's wonderful! How about you and me head down to Walmart later and see what we can do about buying some butterflies."

I can't
diminish
the grin
on my face
as she passes me
my drink.

"Now, how about some sunshine?"

Gladly, I oblige.

Happy to enjoy
the taste of sunshine
once
again.

43.

Our trip
to Walmart
has now become
a family affair.

It's not much,
but I guess it's
something different,
somewhere different.

Courtney put on her lipstick
and that same old
crop top.
Mrs. Lee took
one
look at her.
She knew enough to head back upstairs
and put on something
that
actually resembled
a shirt,
though she kept the lipstick.
I put on
Dad's flannel
again.

Jerm
was the first one
at the door.
He tried to play it cool,
but I could tell he was excited.
First in line
for our
big
trip.

I wonder
if I should feel

sorry for us.

For the
immense excitement
a trip to Walmart
brought,
or say
the hell with it,
and enjoy the trip
for what it would be.

Togetherness

Joy

New beginnings

I decide on the latter.

44.

"Now *that* was one great night!" said Mrs. Lee while unlocking the door.

It really was.

First, we went to McDonalds.
McDouble and fries.
My favorite.

Then we headed
over to
Walmart.
They were out of
butterfly kits,
but there was
a spot for them,
a tag.

They'd be back,
and I'd be waiting.

Sometimes
the best things
are worth the wait.

Like tonight.

There were smiles.

There were laughs.

And it
reminded
 me of
"before."

Only this time,
I was determined

not to take
these moments
for
granted.

45.

Saturday.

A day I used to dread,
but not anymore.

I wake to a robin
playfully singing,
the smell of coffee,
pancakes
and could it possibly be -
bacon!?

I throw on a ratty
but beloved
sweatshirt
from an
old
family vacation,
Rehoboth Beach.

No longer
shying away from the things
that once brought
so much
joy.

Last night,
I pushed past my
well-guarded boundaries
even more.

I figured, why not?

I wasn't exactly crushing it before.

While at Walmart,
I asked Mrs. Lee
if I could buy

a journal.
Our little secret.

I told her
it was to keep
notes about butterflies
for when
we buy
our kit.

A half-truth.

After Dad died,
the school guidance counselor suggested
I keep a journal
to help me
"cope."

At the time,
I'd rather eat glass
than write down my feelings
but now,
I think I might be ready.

Ready to write about family, friendships and forgotten freedoms.

Ready to write about vices and viceroys.

Ready to write about me.

Ready to write.

Ready.

At last.

46.

After science,
I ask Mr. Johnson if there are any
volunteer opportunities
within
the department.

There aren't,
but he tells me about
the school
STEAM club.

Science

Technology

Engineering

Arts

Math

I say thanks,
take the information pamphlet he offers
and walk out the door.
Volunteering is fine,
but I have
no interest
in joining a club.

What STEAM is to me -

Socialization

Teamwork

Excitement

Acceptance

Mirage

Then again,
a few months ago
I had
no interest in butterflies
but here I am,
asking Mr. Johnson
for volunteer opportunities,
writing in a journal
and looking forward to the future.

Metamorphosis.

47.

After dinner and dishes,
which have now become
part of our
nightly routine,
I walk down the hall
past Courtney
and Jeremy's
rooms.

I have to do a double take.

Fully
expecting
to see Jeremy gaming,
I find him sitting at his desk,
book open,
pen in hand.

A smile finds its way to my face.

It seems
I'm not the
only one
who needs Mrs. Lee,
just as much
as she apparently
needs
us.

48.

5/12/22

Dear Diary -

Do people even say that anymore?
I feel silly
writing the words
but don't erase
them
either.

Well, it's been more than a while since the last time I wrote. Soooo much has changed. I don't even know where to begin. It seems like a page, or even five, won't do it justice. Actually, now that I'm thinking about it, that might not be true. Maybe I've been making things more complicated than they are. Maybe, everything can be summed up to one line:

My dad died from cancer.

Mom turned to pills as a way to cope and never learned to separate or deal with the emotions on her own - too scared to think and feel thoughts in their raw form.

Jeremy shut himself off from others and now lives in a make-believe World where he is the controller.

Courtney acts as if nothing happened. She continues to hang out with her friends, ever the social butterfly she always was. I'm starting to wonder if instead of a social butterfly, she's really the viceroy.

And then there's me -

Aware that life will never be what it once was. Aware that what happened to me wasn't fair but also aware that there are many others that have it far worse. Aware that I walk around in a daze, blocking myself off from anything that might cut through my hardened exterior, when what I really want is for someone to give me a hug and hold me when I cry.

I want to be a kid again.

49.

It's been
a couple of weeks
since Mr. Johnson
told me about
STEAM club.

I've kept things
normal enough
with Maddie and Rachel.
Not as hard
as I
once thought.

"Hey, guys. I've got to stay after class today to ask Mr. Johnson a
question. Don't bother waiting. We all know how he can be. Let's just
hope I'm still not here in an hour."

They roll their eyes and wish me luck.

So predictable.

I know exactly what to say and how to say it.

"Hi, Mr. Johnson."

"Hi, Cassie. How are you? Do you have any questions about the
material from today?"

"No, I actually already did the study guide questions and have started
reading ahead."

Mr. Johnson looks surprised
and yet somehow not.

If that's even possible.

"Well, what can I do for you?"

"I've decided I'd like to check out the STEAM club after all. I know it's towards the end of the year, but could I at least attend a meeting sometime?"

He pauses for a moment.
Same look
as before.
How does he keep
demonstrating
this so
well?

The word pops into my head -

Butterfly.

Split in two.

I let
out a
chuckle.

Good ol' dependable Mr. Johnson.

"If you're interested, we'd love to have you join us. We're getting together tomorrow at 3:30 in the Media Center. Hope to see you there."

"Awesome. Thanks so much, Mr. Johnson. See you then."

I basically
run out of
the room,
as if
now that I've dabbled
in this
"new and better life,"
I want to dive in
head first,
shredding all aspects
of the time

I've now decided
to label as
"purgatory."

[Over]compensation should be my middle name.

50.

Back at home,
it's the
"new"
usual scene.

I open the door
to see
Mrs. Lee
in the midst of cooking spaghetti.
Jerm is at the kitchen table.
He has a book open
and is tapping
his pencil
methodically,
brow furrowed,
deep in thought.

Two totally unique
individuals
and Worlds,
yet with
more connection between them
than either
experienced in
years.

It was a welcome sight.

I walk into the kitchen
and ask Jeremy if I can help,
throwing him a life raft
of his own.

51.

The weekend.

Rest.
Relaxation.
Renewal.

I get dressed as usual,
ready for my
"'sunshine in a glass."

I leap down the stairs
but stop dead
in my tracks
at the
bottom step,
afraid to dip my toes in
any further.

I'm not sure
there is enough
sunshine
in the World
to remedy
what's
in sight.

52.

"Hi, sweetie. You look good."

The tremble
in her voice
rivals
the tremble
of my body.

Number 3 has more meaning than ever.

I can tell
she wants to give me a hug,
but my body
is statuesque.

"It's OK. Why don't you go and say hi to your mom," says Mrs. Lee,
gently grabbing my hand and leading me into the kitchen where a giant
glass of orange juice is waiting.

"Hi. When did you get back?"

Relief washes over her body.
She sits down next to me.

"This morning. Honey -

　　　　I roll my tongue in my mouth at the expense of rolling my eyes

I'm so sorry. I don't even know where to begin. I know it's been a
little..."

"A little?" I interrupt. "A week might be a little. It's May. Two months
is not a little."

"I know, and you have every right to be mad at me."

"Don't tell me how to feel."

Tears begin to
silently
stream down my face.
Mrs. Lee sits down next to me,
reaching for my hand
and providing me
with the maternal comfort
my own mother
chose to throw
away.

"I'm so, so sorry. I don't even know what else to say, just that I needed
to get myself straight. This is the last thing I wanted for you, for us, but
I'm clean now. We can be a family again and move forward. I didn't
know how to move forward without your father. It was like I couldn't
breathe, the grief constantly pulling me under. I couldn't care for you,
couldn't care for myself, but I can now, if you'll let me."

I see Mrs. Lee's eyes
travel towards
the stairs again.
When I turn my head
I see Courtney
and Jeremy,
same deer-in-headlights look
I had
moments before.
Courtney just standing there,
phone in hand,
motionless.

I wonder if they feel the same as me.

Not knowing
if they should run into
Mom's arms
or
straight for the door.

Cry happy tears because

she is finally home
or
cry with remorse for the
exact same
reason.

Split in two.

I wipe the tears from my eyes,
stand up from the table
and walk out the door,
simply saying
I need some
air.

My life seems to be a ball of uncertainty.

Woven together
with cheap thread,
that if pulled from
any direction
would ravel
apart.

However,
I do know one thing.
I can say with
100% certainty
I would
not have reacted
as calmly
to my mother's homecoming
two months prior.

Progress.

Regression
whisked away
with Mom.

I won't let it return with her arrival.

53.

When I'm back home
two hours later,
Mrs. Lee is sitting
at the
kitchen table,
reading a book.

Mom isn't around.

After her reunion with
Jeremy and Courtney
went about
as well as mine,
she decided to give us
some time to
"think."

"Come here, darling," said Mrs. Lee.

I walk slowly over to the table.
I want to crumble into
Mrs. Lee's arms,
relieved to see the face
of someone who
feels like home.

But what did Mom's return mean for her?

"There, there, sweetheart. It's OK. However you feel right now, it's all
OK."

"Did you know she was coming?"

"I had no idea. I woke up this morning and went about my day like
normal. I heard a tapping at the door, looked over and saw your mom
standing there. My body became as immobile as yours. Cas, I love you
like you're my own daughter. You children have given my life meaning

again. You brought laughter and love to my lonely heart. But we both knew this was only until your mother came home."

"But can't you stay? It's not fair! She took off and left you to pick up the pieces! You healed me, Jeremy and Courtney. YOU! As far as I'm concerned, you're a far better mother than she ever was."

"Cas, I don't think you really mean that."

She always knows.

I want to mean it,
but she wasn't always
a bad mom.
People can change.
I have.

"Your mom left *for* you. She knew it was you or the pills, and she chose you. She will always choose you. And when you feel sad or alone, know that *I* will always choose you. You and your family have been the greatest gift I could ever receive."

At this point,
we are both
crying so hard
tears are dripping
onto the tablecloth.

Raw and exposed, all defenses removed.

I know she's right.
The arrangement was always temporary.

Why do some of life's greatest blessings have to fly away?

I think
I've let go of more butterflies
in my 15 years
than most people have
in 55.

What is it they say?

"If you love something, set it free?"

I'm not so sure
the person who wrote that ever
truly lost something
or someone
they loved.
It's like an appendage
gets ripped off.
You learn to live with it,
yet always aware of its absence.

Is that better than the alternative?

The jury's still out.

54.

I look out the window
at the sound of
my alarm.

Sunny.

What I've become accustomed to.

I sit here,
waiting for the clouds
to take
over.

I smell pancakes.

Did Mrs. Lee decide to stay?

I bound down the stairs,
but at the bottom of the steps
I see my
mom.

Trying

Sweating

Staring intently at the
pancake batter
while biting her lower lip,
as if cooking these pancakes
will be the most
important thing
she'll ever do.

I look at the table
and see a glass of orange juice.

Mrs. Lee must have told her.

Maybe the clouds
won't pass
after
all.

55.

I go outside
for an
afternoon walk,
hoping to run into
Mrs. Lee.

She's in her garden.

"Hi, Cas!" she calls, obvious excitement in her voice.

"Hi, Mrs. Lee."

I kneel down next to her
and help weed
the flowers
she somehow
managed to tend,
all while tending
to us.

No words necessary,
an understanding
fills the air.

An understanding of loss.

An understanding of love.

An understanding of acceptance.

An understanding of growth.

An understanding of forgiveness.

For the first time
I understand how
gardening
can be soothing,

poetic even.

I slowly
get up to leave,
pat the dirt
off my knees
and begin to walk away,
knowing this
will be our last encounter
for some time.

Both of us
needing to
figure out this
new life
on our
own.

"Cas."

"Yes?"

"Please don't forget about the butterflies. I expect to know when you
buy your kit."

A sledgehammer couldn't break the bond between us.

56.

A few weeks have passed,
and I'm still
able to
float.

My friends didn't notice
anything
out of the norm.

A viceroy in sheep's skin.

Jeremy is now back in school consistently.
Courtney's still Courtney
but slightly toned down,
and I am now
regularly attending
STEAM club.

Mom thinks it's a great idea.
An outlet for me
to
"express myself,"
new journeys to take.

A purpose in my new life.

Giving purpose to hers.

57.

"Good afternoon, class. Please take your seats."

"As you all know, the end of the school year is approaching. We have learned all about the life cycle of a butterfly, climate, population, statistics and everything you are "expected" to learn in class. However, if you recall, at the start of the unit I discussed the term metamorphosis. I've graded your assignments, and the academic portion of the unit is complete. What I want to know is how this unit impacted you personally, if at all. For your final assignment, I want you to turn in a response to that question. There is no requirement for page count, style and no right/wrong answer."

The class stared at him
in awe,
shocked that Mr. Johnson
of all teachers
would assign a project
with so much
freedom.

With a slight grin he said, "What? Even the tallest of trees continue to grow."

58.

Back in my room,
I pull out
my pen and paper.
It's been three days
since Mr. Johnson
gave us
our final assignment,
and I still haven't put
more than
my name
at the
top of the
page.

So easy to write my name,
yet impossible to fill in the details.

The paper is due tomorrow,
so I force myself to write.

Surprisingly,
once I get started
the words bounce
from
head to
pen to
page,
creating a life
of their own.

Mr. Johnson,

When you first assigned a project on butterflies, I found it quite juvenile. I thought I had learned the basics and that this was just another typical, boring unit. I was so very wrong.

What you may or may not know, is that while we have been learning about butterflies, my life has been in complete disarray. My mom left

113

for an extended period of time, our family is still adjusting to the death of my father, and I have been trying to find my place in the World and in my family ever since. That's why I asked you about the viceroy, specifically. I can picture myself as that butterfly, chaotically trying to pass myself off as anything but what I am, afraid to be myself. This is the life I felt resigned to lead.

Our first thought question was about the definition of the word "butterfly." Of all the thought questions, this one resonated the most. Here is the short answer:

1. *I am not a "social butterfly." The thought of needing a group or unit always seemed foreign to me, especially after my dad's passing. If there were any thought of being part of a group or social club, it was definitely before then. But since our introduction to butterflies, I have now found myself in a club with people I can't wait to see at the end of each day. I learned that, maybe, I need to be a "social butterfly" as much as I need my solitude.*

2. *I easily connected with the term "butterflies in your stomach." Butterflies kicked around my stomach from the minute my mom told me she was leaving for a few days, which turned into more than a few weeks. Don't worry, I was being taken care of by a neighbor who has since become so much more. Unfortunately, when you are a child and forced to face "adult" situations, "butterflies in your stomach" become an unwelcome friend.*

3. *The verb form of butterfly, to split in two, also took on new importance during this time. A constant juxtaposition in regards to my mom: love/hate; disapproval/understanding; detachment/need. Never-ending.*

4. *The definition I struggled with the most was the noun form of the word - how could I relate to brightly-colored, erect wings and dilated antennae? As this unit and school year come to a close, I can finally find a relation between myself and the butterfly, not only the viceroy. I now see the color in myself and in the sky when I look outside. I am proud of who I am and have begun to see the World through those eyes, which are finally ready to receive whatever is ahead.*

In closing, I learned about butterflies this year, but I learned about life; about survival; and about myself.

The most difficult and rewarding lesson of all.

Cassie

EPILOGUE

The day after turning in her letter to Mr. Johnson, Cassie walked over to Mrs. Lee's house, newly purchased butterfly kit in hand.

Following the initial excitement and hugs, they opened up the kit and became lost in the dreams they once created together. It was an experience that solidified the bond they would forever share.

It began with just Cassie and Mrs. Lee, but by the time the caterpillars had begun to change into chrysalises, Jeremy and Courtney were coming over for regular visits, joining in the brilliance of self-preservation and change. They all needed that, and the experience signified an end to the times of "before" and "purgatory," both necessary for their metamorphosis.

Within the three weeks it took for the caterpillars to turn into butterflies, Cassie's mom started participating in the process. It took time for Cassie, Jeremy and Courtney to trust she would stay, but if caterpillars could trust that something beautiful would come from their unexpected journey, so could they.

Gathered together, they excitedly waited to release their butterflies into the air. A family unlike any other, who persevered through the odds. Still figuring things out, but for the first time, hopeful for the future. When they let the butterflies go, Cassie watched their beautiful wings, erect and ready for the unknown adventures yet to be discovered.

Those butterflies, finally grown enough to go out into the World as the best and most beautiful versions of themselves.

Endless opportunities awaited, awaited them all.

Their transformation now complete, there they stood, ready to take flight.

Sandra Whiting is a poet and author from Western, NY. She is employed as a Speech-Language Pathologist and teaches kids yoga classes in her spare time. Two of Sandra's poems, "I Believe in Magic" and "The Coolest Cat in Town" can be found on The Dirigible Balloon.

Made in the USA
Columbia, SC
11 July 2023

20265662R00065